Magic Story-box

Senior Author
John A. McInnes

Associate Authors
Margaret Gerrard
John Ryckman

Contents

Magic Story~box~ Open with care

"Get down," said the little polar bear.
"It's time for us to hide."

"Come on," said the pink gorilla.
"We all must squeeze inside."

"I'm squeezing," said the octopus,
and wiggled as she did.

"Don't squash me," said the meadow mouse,
who cuddled down and hid.

"I hear the children coming,"
said the cow that jumped the moon.
"Remember what you have to do—
they're going to find us soon."

"We know," they said together.
"We'll make the children smile.
We might even try to scare them
for just a little while.
We'll let them get to know us,
and let them take a look
in all our secret corners
when they come inside our book."

John McInnes

5

The Wishing Well

Grandfather Elf

Once upon a time there was a little old elf. He lived in a house in the woods. He was friends with all the animals. They called him Grandfather Elf.

Every morning Grandfather Elf went for a walk in the woods. He went to see his friends and talk to them. Sometimes he took Googie Mouse for a walk. Sometimes he helped Mrs. Rabbit with her little rabbits. And sometimes he showed Froggie Frog where to find good things to eat.

One morning Grandfather Elf did not go for a walk in the woods. All the animals were surprised.

"Where is Grandfather Elf this morning?" they all asked.

No one had seen him.

"I'll go and look for him," said Googie Mouse. Away he went to the old elf's house. When he got there, Googie knocked on the door.

Knock! Knock! Knock!

"Grandfather Elf, are you in there?" called Googie.

"Yes," answered the elf.

"Are you going for your walk today?" asked Googie.

"Not today," answered Grandfather Elf. "I am sick in bed."

"May I come in?" asked Googie.

"Yes, Googie," answered Grandfather Elf. "Come on in."

Googie opened the door and walked in. Grandfather Elf was in bed.

"Oh dear!" said Googie when he saw Grandfather Elf. "You don't look very well. Can I get you something to eat?"

"No thanks, Googie," said Grandfather Elf. "I don't feel like eating."

Googie did not know what to do. "I'll go and ask Mrs. Rabbit," he said to himself. "Maybe she can help."

Googie ran as fast as he could to Mrs. Rabbit's house. When he got there, the door was open. He looked in.

"Mrs. Rabbit! Mrs. Rabbit!" called Googie.

"What is it?" said Mrs. Rabbit. "Did you find Grandfather Elf?"

"Yes," said Googie. "He is sick and he cannot get out of bed. What are we going to do?"

"Let me see," said Mrs. Rabbit. "When my little rabbits are not feeling well, I give them cookies to eat. Maybe I could take some cookies to Grandfather Elf."

"He said he did not feel like eating," said Googie.

"Then I know what to do," said Mrs. Rabbit. "We will get Froggie Frog to help. When Froggie Frog was sick he went to the wishing well. He made a wish and he got better. We could take Grandfather Elf to the wishing well."

"He's too sick to go to the wishing well," said Googie.

"Then we will have to go to the well for him," said Mrs. Rabbit.

"But I don't know where the well is," said Googie. "Do you?"

"No," answered Mrs. Rabbit. "But Froggie knows. We will go and find him."

Mrs. Rabbit said to the little rabbits, "Grandfather Elf is not feeling well. Googie and I want to help him, but first we are going to look for Froggie Frog. Eat your cookies like good little rabbits, and don't go away from the house. We will be back soon."

Mrs. Rabbit and Googie went to look for Froggie Frog. They looked everywhere, but they could not find him.

"Froggie," called Mrs. Rabbit.

"Where are you, Froggie?" called Googie.

"Froggie! Froggie!" they called again and again.

"Oh dear," said Googie. "Where can he be?"

Mrs. Rabbit said, "If we don't find him soon I don't know what we are going to do!"

A Very Good Wish

Googie and Mrs. Rabbit looked for Froggie Frog for a long time. Just when they were about to give up, they heard a splash.

"Did you hear that?" asked Mrs. Rabbit.

"Yes, I heard it," said Googie. "Let's go and see if it's Froggie."

Away they went. They came to the water.

Splash! Splash!

They looked. It was a big fish.

"Oh dear," said Googie, "If we don't find Froggie Frog, we will never find the well. If we don't find the well, we can't make a wish."

"If we can't make a wish, then Grandfather Elf may never get better," said Mrs. Rabbit.

Splash!

What a surprise! There was Froggie Frog.

"Did I hear you say that Grandfather Elf may never get better?" said Froggie. "I did not know he was sick."

"Oh, yes," said Googie. "He's very sick."

"We want to go to the well to make a wish for him," said Mrs. Rabbit. "Will you take us there?"

"Oh,yes," said Froggie. "Once when I was feeling sick Grandfather Elf helped me. He went to the wishing well and made a wish for me. All at once I got better. Let's go to the well and make a wish for Grandfather Elf."

Away went the three friends. Soon they came to an open place in the woods.

"Look!" said Googie. "There's the wishing well."

"What do we do now?" asked Mrs. Rabbit.

"One of you will have to make a wish," said Froggie. "You go up to the well and look down into the water. When you can see the water, the water can see you. Then you make your wish."

"May I make the wish?" asked Googie. "I want to help Grandfather Elf."

"We all want to help Grandfather Elf," said Mrs. Rabbit, "but you may be the one to make the wish."

Googie went up to the well and looked down. He saw the water and the water saw him.

"Make the wish, Googie," called Froggie.

Before Googie could make his wish, the wishing well said, "Why are you here? What do you want? Are you going to make a good wish?"

"Yes," said Googie. "I have a good wish. It's not for myself. It's for Grandfather Elf. He could not come here."

"Why not?" asked the well.

"He's sick in bed," said Googie. "Please help him get better. That's my wish."

Splash! went the water in the well.

"That was a good wish, Googie Mouse," said the well. "You made a wish to help a friend. I'm going to give you your wish. Grandfather Elf is feeling better now."

"Oh, thank you, Wishing Well," said Googie. "Thank you! Thank you!"

Googie called to Mrs. Rabbit and Froggie. "I have my wish! Grandfather Elf is feeling better now! Let's all go and see him!"

Froggie and Mrs. Rabbit were very happy to hear the news.

Away they all went to Grandfather Elf's house. Googie got there first. Froggie came second. Mrs. Rabbit was third. She had stopped on the way for some cookies.

Googie knocked on the door. Grandfather Elf opened it.

He said, "Mrs. Rabbit and Froggie and Googie! I'm so glad to see you. I'm feeling better now!"

"Yes, we know!" said the three friends.

"You do?" asked Grandfather Elf.

"Yes," said Googie. "We went to the wishing well, and I wished for you to get better, and the well said I could have my wish."

"Thank you, friends," said Grandfather Elf. "I'm glad I have friends like you."

"And now," said Mrs. Rabbit, "it's time to have something to eat. I have cookies for everyone."

They ate all the cookies. Grandfather Elf was feeling so well he had three.

"Now I will go and thank the well," he said.

"We will come with you," said Froggie Frog.

"Then we can have our walk in the woods," said Googie.

A Big Bad Wish

There was one animal in the woods that no one liked. He was a big wolf, and all the animals were scared of him. When the wolf went walking in the woods, he would shout,

"I am a wolf,
A big bad wolf
As bad as I can be.
I am a wolf,
A big bad wolf,
Come here and look at me."

When Googie and his friends heard the wolf, they would run away as fast as they could.

Every day, Mrs. Rabbit said to her little rabbits, "Don't go too far away from home. If you do, the big bad wolf will eat you up."

And every day the little rabbits said to their mother, "We will look out for the wolf. We know he will eat us up if he finds us."

One morning, the wolf was walking in the woods. He saw something that he had never seen before. He stopped and looked at it.

"This looks like the wishing well," he said. "I have heard about it. It can talk and give you your wish."

The wolf went up to the well and looked down at the water. "Wishing Well," he said, "talk to me."

The well did not answer. Then the wolf shouted, "I am a big bad wolf. Talk to me. I know you can hear me."

The well made a little splash. "Is someone there?" asked the well.

"Yes," answered the wolf, "I'm here!"

"Who are you?" asked the well.

The wolf shouted,
"I am a wolf,
A big bad wolf,
I'm bad as I can be.
I am a wolf,
A big bad wolf,
Give my wish to me!"

The wishing well splashed and said, "I can't hear very well. Jump up on me and tell me who you are once again."

The wolf jumped up. "Who am I?" he shouted. "Everyone knows who I am. I am the big bad wolf!"

"Oh," said the well, "I see. You are the big bad wolf. Why are you here? Do you want some water?"

"No," said the wolf, "I don't want water. I want my wish, and I want it now!"

"A wish?" asked the well. "Is it a good wish? Are you wishing for something good?"

"Yes, yes," shouted the wolf. "I want something good to eat."

"Do you want some apples?" asked the well. "Apples are good for you."

"No, no!" cried the wolf. "I don't want apples."

The well said, "I am very old. I cannot hear very well, and I cannot see very well. If I cannot see you, I cannot give you your wish. Look away down here. Now tell me once again. What do you want? What is your wish?"

The big bad wolf looked away down the well and showed his teeth. "I want something good to eat," he shouted. "I want to eat Mrs. Rabbit and all her little rabbits. Make them come here at once. I have a big surprise for them."

"I heard you that time," said the well. "You have a big surprise for the rabbits. And I have a big surprise for you. Are you ready?"

"Yes," answered the wolf, "I'm ready."

Splash! Splash! Splash!

Up came the water. Down went the wolf into the well.

"Help! Help!" he cried. "Get me out of here! Wishing Well! Wishing Well! Do what I tell you."

The wishing well did not answer.

"Help! Help!" the wolf cried again. "If you don't help me, I'll never get out!"

The well made a splash. It was like a little laugh.

"Please don't laugh at me," cried the wolf. "I know I made a bad wish. I want to get out. I'm scared."

"Good," said the wishing well. "That is just what I wanted to hear. Tell me that you will never scare the animals again. Then make your wish."

"I will never scare the animals again," said the wolf. "I wish to get out of here."

Splash! Splash! Splash!

Out of the well came the wolf. Away he ran as fast as he could go. As he ran, he said to himself,

> "I am a wolf,
> A big good wolf,
> As good as I can be.
> I am a wolf,
> A big good wolf,
> The wishing well scared me."

Wish, Wish, Wish

Wish, wish, wish at the magic wishing well,
You may get your wishes, but you never can tell.
Googie got a good wish
        for his friend, the elf,
Wolfie made a bad one –
        nearly drowned himself!
Wish, wish, wish at the magic wishing well,
You may get your wishes, but you never can tell.
Ask for something super, scrumptious, or delish,
But don't take any chances
On a big, bad wish.

John McInnes

Magic Pet

I have a silly magic pet,
It came one summer day.
I had no place to keep it
But it wouldn't go away.

It fed itself on chocolate cake
And hung from chandeliers,
It ran to answer telephones
Then stuck them in its ears.

It carved its name on table tops,
It ruined my guitar.
It ate up all my cookies
Then broke the cookie jar.

And that is why it's come to this—
I said it had to leave.
It disobeyed, and what is more
It now lives up my sleeve.

Clayton Graves

Jeremy Jay and Gogo

My name is Jeremy Jay and I have a pet gorilla. Some gorillas are big and black, but my gorilla is big and pink. I call him Gogo.

Gogo lives at my house. He has his very own room. He has his very own bed and his very own toys.

Sometimes Gogo and I play in my room with my toys. I have building bricks. Gogo likes to build houses with them. Sometimes we play in his room with his toys. Gogo has a jack-in-the-box. He makes it jump up and surprise me. It surprises him, too.

Every morning Gogo comes into my room and gets me out of bed so we can go for a walk before school. He puts on his big straw hat, and I put on my little one. Then off we go.

Sometimes I take Gogo for a walk. Sometimes he takes me for a walk. When we get home from our walk, I get ready for school.

On Saturdays I can be with Gogo all day. I like Saturdays.

One Saturday, Gogo put on his big straw hat. I put on my straw hat, too. We went to the circus. Some of our friends were there. They were happy to see us.

It wasn't a very big circus. They had one elephant, two bears, and three clowns. The elephant walked into the circus ring and sat down. The bears played with a red ball. Then the clowns came out.

The first clown shouted at the elephant. All the elephant did was sit there. It was not a very funny act. No one laughed.

The second clown jumped in and out of a big box. She was not very funny. No one laughed at her.

The third clown bumped into things. His act was not funny at all.

All at once one of my friends called out, "We want Gogo! We want Gogo!"

Soon everyone at the circus was calling, "We want Gogo! We want Gogo!"

Everyone wanted Gogo to do his tricks.

One of the circus men called to me, "Is that your pink gorilla? Is that Gogo?"

"Yes," I answered, "this is Gogo."

"Can he do tricks?" asked the man.

"Yes! Yes! Yes!" called my friends.

"Come down into the ring and show us," said the man.

Gogo and I went down into the ring.

I said to Gogo, "Let's show everyone what you can do."

Gogo jumped up on the elephant's back. The elephant began to walk. Up and down the ring it went with Gogo on its back.

Then Gogo took a big red ball and walked on it. He made two bears get up on chairs and do tricks. He jumped in and out of boxes. He bumped into things and put on funny hats. Everyone laughed and laughed.

At the end of Gogo's act we went out of the ring. The circus man said to me, "Little boy, I want your gorilla for my circus. Will you sell him to me?"

I looked at the man. "Sell Gogo?" I said. "Never! Some day I may have a circus of my own. Then Gogo can do tricks in my circus."

When we got home, I said to Gogo, "I'll never sell you. Every morning we can go for walks before I go to school. We will play with our toys and have fun doing tricks. You are not just a pet. You are my friend."

Jeremy Jay and Boo-Hoo

On Saturday mornings Gogo and I go for long walks. We like to find new places to go. I'm not scared to go far from home when Gogo is with me.

One Saturday morning I put on my new yellow boots. Gogo put on his new boots, too. We went for a walk in the woods. We liked our walk. There were lots of things for us to see.

All at once we heard something.

Boo-hoo! Boo-hoo!

"What can that be?" I said to Gogo. "Let's go and see."

We heard it again. It was not far away. "I know where to look," I said. "Let's go this way."

Just then we saw a big brown bird. He was on a log. He was crying.

Boo-hoo! Boo-hoo!

Gogo and I had never seen a bird like that before.

"Hello, bird," I said. "My name is Jeremy Jay and this is Gogo. What is your name?"

"Boo-hoo!" said the bird.

"Why are you crying?" I asked.

"I'm on this log and I can't get off," said the bird.

"Well," I said. "You are a bird. Why don't you fly off the log?"

"I can't," said the bird. "I don't know how to fly. Boo-hoo!"

"Stop crying," I said. "Tell me how you got on the log in the first place."

The bird told us his story.

"I was walking in the woods and I lost my way. I got up on this log and looked all about. I began to cry. I cried and cried. Soon there was water everywhere. Then you came along. It's no fun to be on this log. I want to get off. Boo-hoo! Boo-hoo!"

"Don't cry," I said. "Just walk in the water."

"Oh, no," cried the bird. "I can't do that. I don't want to get my feet wet."

"Gogo and I will help you," I said.

Just then Gogo jumped up on the log. He sat down with the bird and took off his new yellow boots.

"Put on Gogo's boots," I said to the bird. "Then you will not get your feet wet."

"Thank you, Gogo," said the bird. He put on Gogo's yellow boots.

Gogo jumped off the log. The bird walked into the water. When he came out of the water he said, "Boo-hoo! Boo-hoo!"

"Why are you crying now?" I asked. "You got off the log and you did not get your feet wet."

"Oh yes," said the bird. "Now I'm so happy I could cry. Boo-hoo! Boo-hoo!"

"Why don't you stop crying and come with us," I said. "We are going home. You can live at my house. We can go for walks every day. We will get you some boots of your own. You will never get your feet wet and you will never get lost again. We will be friends."

Home we went—the three of us.

Would You Like Me For a Pet?

orangoutang

polar bear

deer

tiger   snowy owl

alligator   zebra

penguins

I Dream Stories

I dream stories that I've never read
Almost every night when I go to bed.
Fantastic things happen in my room
Elephants dance and rockets zoom.
Every dream's special, or so it seems,
That's why I like my story dreams.
They're better than anything on TV,
Because they're mine; they're made for me.

John McInnes

Dream Stories

One morning in school, Elizabeth said, "I had a funny dream Saturday night. I went to the moon."

"How did you get there?" asked Ted.

"I'm not going to tell you now," answered Elizabeth. "I'm going to make some pictures first. Then I'll tell you a story about my dream. I'll put myself in the pictures and in the story."

"I had a dream, too," said Susan. "In my dream, I was playing with Gus. We went for a ride, but we did not go to the moon."

"Where did we go?" asked Gus.

"I'll tell you if you will help me make some pictures about my dream," answered Susan.

"I would like that," said Gus. "I'll get some paper and some paint. You can tell me what pictures to make. Then you can write the dream story about us."

Elizabeth asked Nick, "Did you have a dream, too?"

"One time my dad came home from the lake with some fish," said Nick. "My cat, Mittens, took one of them and hid it under my bed. When I went to bed, I had a dream about Mittens and the fish. It was a funny dream. Do you want to hear about it?"

"Not just now," said Elizabeth. "Why don't you write your story and then read it to us?"

"I will," said Nick. "You will like it. I'll be in the story and so will Mittens."

"We can show our pictures and read our stories when we are ready," said Elizabeth. "They will be about us."

"Maybe we can put our dream stories in a big book for all our friends to read," said Susan.

"We can put our dream pictures in the book, too," said Ted.

"Yes, that will be fun," said Nick. "We can call the book, *Dream Stories*."

Elizabeth's Dream
Toot-toot

Once upon a time there was a little girl called Elizabeth. She had a dream about her toy train.

In her dream she said to herself, "I wish I were so small that I could get into my toy train."

All at once, she got her wish. Before she could get into the train it said, "Toot-toot! Hello, Elizabeth. Do you want to go for a ride?"

"Oh yes, please," said Elizabeth. "I'd like to go for a ride. Where are you going?"

"Where do you want to go?" asked the train. "I can go everywhere. I am a magic train. Toot-toot!"

"If you can go everywhere, then I'd like to go to the moon," said Elizabeth.

"Jump in," said the train. "I'm ready to go now. Toot-toot!"

Elizabeth got into the train and sat down.

Zoom! Zoom! Zoom!
Up and up it went.

Elizabeth looked out the window.
The train was going so fast that she could not
see her own house. She liked going fast.

"Where are we going?" asked Elizabeth.

"You wanted to go to the moon and that is
where we are going," said the train.

"Good," said Elizabeth. "That is where I
want to go. Will it take a long time to get
there?"

"No," answered the train. "I can get there in
no time at all. Toot-toot!"

The little train zoomed on and on, and up and
up.

Elizabeth looked out the window of the train
again.

"This is fun," she said. "I wish that all my
friends could see me now. They would like to
be with me."

All at once there was a big bump. The train stopped. "Here we are," said the train. "Out you get. Toot-toot!"

Elizabeth looked out the window. "Well, well," she said. "I wanted to go to the moon and here I am."

She opened the door and got out.

All at once she saw a little man with a red hat.

"Are you the man in the moon?" she asked.

"No," he answered, "but I will take you to him."

On the Moon

Elizabeth had never seen a place like this before. The moon was not yellow. It was gray and black. There were no trees. There were no houses. There were no animals. She looked all about.

"There must be something on the moon," she said to herself.

Just then she saw a funny old man. He had a yellow nose. He had yellow hair and yellow whiskers. He was all yellow!

"Hello," said Elizabeth. "You must be the man in the moon."

"I am the man in the moon," he said "I have never seen you before. Who are you?"

"My name is Elizabeth," she said. "I wanted to come to the moon. I came in my toy train."

"Do you want to see my moon?" he asked.

"Oh, yes," answered Elizabeth.

The man in the moon took Elizabeth for a walk. He showed her things that she had never seen before.

All at once Elizabeth looked up. "What is that?" she asked.

"A cow," answered the man in the moon.

"She must be the cow that jumps over the moon," said Elizabeth. "I have heard about her."

"A long time ago I had lots of cows," said the man in the moon. "They could all jump over the moon. Now I have just one cow and she is very old."

"I'm so glad I saw her," said Elizabeth.

Just then the train called, "Toot-toot! Come, Elizabeth, you have seen the moon. Now it's time to go home."

"Good-bye, Elizabeth," said the man in the moon. "Come up and see me again some time."

"Good-bye," called Elizabeth. "Thank you for showing me the moon."

Then Elizabeth got into the train.

Toot-toot! Zoom! Zoom! Down, down it went!

When the train stopped, Elizabeth got out. "Thanks," she said to the toy train. "I can tell all my friends I have been to the moon."

"Toot-toot," said the train.

Elizabeth got out of the toy train.

"It was fun to go to the moon," said Elizabeth. "Now that I'm home, I wish I were big again."

And all at once she was!

Hey Diddle Diddle

Hey, diddle, diddle!
The cat and the fiddle,
The cow jumped over the moon.
The little dog laughed
To see such sport,
And the dish ran away with the spoon.

Susan's Dream
The Magic Bus

One night Susan had a dream about herself and her friend, Gus. In the dream they were walking down their street when they saw a very funny bus. It stopped near them.

"Do you want to go for a ride in this bus?" asked Susan.

"Oh, yes," answered Gus. "I have never been on a bus like this one."

The driver opened the door and the children got on the bus. What a surprise they had. The driver was a big green fish!

Zoom! Away went the bus. Susan and Gus were scared but they could not get off. The bus was going very fast. It went up hills and down hills. It went into the woods and came out of the woods. It went on and on.

"Where do you think we are going?" asked Gus.

"I don't know," answered Susan.

Gus said, "I'll go and ask the driver, if you'll come with me."

The children talked to the fish. "Where are we going, Bus Driver?" asked Gus.

"We are going under the water," answered the fish.

"Why?" asked Susan.

"I want to show you some beautiful things in the sea," said the fish.

"We are not fish!" said Gus. "We can't go under the sea."

"Yes, you can," said the driver. "You'll see. This is a magic bus. It can take us under the sea."

Just then, the magic bus came to the water. It did not stop. It went down under the water.

Under the Sea

The bus went on and on. Susan and Gus looked out the window. Sometimes the sea looked blue. Then it looked green.

What beautiful things there were under the sea!

A school of little fish came along. A big blue fish was after them.

"Look over there at the big fish," said Susan. "It's going to eat the little fish."

The little fish saw the big fish just in time. They got away.

Then the driver said, "I'm going to show you some little horses."

"Horses!" said Susan. "I have never heard of horses that live under water."

"They must be magic horses," said Gus.

"No," said the driver. "They are sea horses. They live under the water all the time. Look, there they are. What do you think of them?"

Gus said, "I think they are very beautiful."

"I would like to have a ride on one," said Susan.

"You are too big," laughed Gus.

Just then, Susan shouted, "Look out, everyone! Something is after us."

Two big eyes looked in at them.

"Help! Help!" cried Gus.

"It's just an octopus," said the driver. "You don't have to be scared."

"But it's so big," said Gus.

"Is it one of your friends?" asked Susan.

"Yes," answered the fish. "It wants a ride on my bus. But I will take you home first. Here we go!"

Soon the bus came out of the water. It went into the woods. It went down hills and up hills. Susan and Gus were glad when the bus went down their street. It stopped just where they had got on.

"Is this a dream?" Susan asked Gus.

"What do you think?" asked Gus.

Nick's Dream

One night Nick had a dream about his cat. In his dream Mittens wanted some fish. Nick looked and looked, but there were no fish in the house.

"I know what we can do," said Nick. "We can go to the lake and get you some fish."

Nick took Mittens to the lake. They went fishing.

They fished for a long time but they did not get any fish. All at once they saw a little white bear. He was fishing, too.

"Look at the little bear over there," said Nick. "Do you think he is getting any fish? I will ask him."

"Hello, Little Bear," called Nick. "How is the fishing over there?"

"Grrr," said the little bear. "There are no fish in this lake. I'm going home. The fishing is better there."

"We are ready to go home, too," said Nick. "My cat is sad. She likes fish and we did not get any."

"Why don't you come home with me?" asked the little bear. "We have lots of fish at my house."

"Where do you live?" asked Nick.

"I live far away from here," answered the little bear, "but it will not take long to get there."

"Mittens and I would like to go with you," said Nick.

"I can take you in my car," said the little bear. "There's lots of room. My car takes me anywhere I want to go," said the little bear. "It's magic. I make a wish and away I go."

They all got into the magic car. The little bear made a wish. The car took off and went like the wind. Nick could not see where they were going.

After a time, the car stopped. Nick looked out the window. There was snow everywhere.

"Here we are," said the little bear. "Come with me. My mother will give you some fish."

"It looks cold out there," said Nick. "I don't have a coat. I can't come with you."

I'll make a wish for you, before we get out of the magic car," said the little bear. "I wish you had a coat."

All at once Nick had on a white coat with a hood. He was surprised.

"How do I look?" asked Nick.

"Just like a bear," answered Nick's new friend.

The bear took Nick home with him.

Mother Bear looked at Nick. "I have never seen this little bear before," she said. "Who is he?"

The little bear laughed and said, "He's not a bear, he's a little boy."

"Where did you find him?" asked Mother Bear.

"Far, far away," answered the little bear. "He was fishing at the lake near his home. He could not get any fish so I asked him to come with me. Will you give him some fish?"

"Yes," said the mother bear. "Would you like to eat one now?"

"No thanks," said Nick. "I'll take them to Mittens. She's in the car."

"Mittens must be a little boy, too," said the mother bear.

"Oh, no," laughed Nick. "Mittens is my cat."

When Nick got back to the car, Mittens was glad to see him. Mittens was glad to see the fish, too.

"Mew," said Mittens and she ate the fish.

"We must be going now," said Nick. "How will we get home?"

"I'll take you in the magic car," said the little bear. "Get in with me."

Nick got into the car. He took off the coat.
The little bear made a wish. The car took off
and went like the wind. Soon they were at
Nick's house. The little bear said good-bye, and
away he went in his car.

"Well, Mittens," said Nick, "you never can tell
what will happen when you go fishing."

"Mew," said Mittens, as she ate some more
fish.

Magic Rides

My magic train
Goes any place.
Zoom!
I'm off to outer space.

My magic bus
Surprises me.
Splash!
I'm underneath the sea.

My magic car
Goes everywhere.
I make a wish!
It takes me there.

Let's Go For A Ride

balloon

stage coach

snowmobile

helicopter

paddle steamer

carousel

circus ride

What Next?

"It was fun to make up dream stories," said Susan. "What are we going to do next?"

"We have read lots of stories about animals," said Nick. "We could make up a play about them. Then we could have Gogo the gorilla, and the boo-hoo bird in the play."

Kim said, "We could have Googie and Froggie and Mrs. Rabbit in it, too."

"After we write the play, we will have to make things for it," said Gus.

"And we'll have to put make-up on our faces," said Susan.

"It would be better to make animal masks," said Elizabeth.

"It would be funny if the animals in our play put on a show," said Susan. "Let's get to work."

The children worked on the play. Soon they were ready to put it on.

The Stars of the Show

CAST: Mrs. Rabbit, Googie, Froggie, Gogo, Boo-Hoo, Little Bear, and Wolf.

Act One

*(*MRS. RABBIT *and* GOOGIE *are on stage.)*

MRS. RABBIT: It's Friday, Googie. It's the day of the show, and we are not ready yet. We must see everyone who wants to be in the show.

GOOGIE: I will call them out on stage, one at a time. We'll see what they can do. Froggie, come out on stage. You can be first.

(FROGGIE *comes in.*)

MRS. RABBIT: Hello, Froggie. Are you ready? What are you going to do?

FROGGIE: I'm going to jump over three boxes. That's my act. Here I go.

(FROGGIE *jumps over the three boxes.*)

MRS. RABBIT: That's very good, Froggie. You can be in the show.

FROGGIE: I wish I could be the star of the show.

MRS. RABBIT: We'll see about that. Good-bye, Froggie.

(FROGGIE *goes out.*)

MRS. RABBIT: Will you please call the next one, Googie?

GOOGIE: Gogo! Gogo! It's your turn.

(GOGO *comes in.*)

MRS. RABBIT: Show us what you can do.

GOGO: Here I am, everyone. I make funny faces. Just look at me. Here's my first funny face.

(GOGO *makes a funny face.*)

MRS. RABBIT: Ha! Ha! Ha! You make me laugh. You are very funny. Can you make another funny face?

GOGO: I can make lots of funny faces.
(GOGO makes funny faces.)

GOOGIE and
MRS. RABBIT: Ha! Ha! Ha! Ha! Ha! Ha! Ha!
Hee! Hee! Hee! Hee!

MRS. RABBIT: You are very funny, Gogo. You can be in our show.

GOGO: I wish I could be the star of the show.

MRS. RABBIT: We'll see about that. Good-bye, Gogo.

(GOGO goes out.)

MRS. RABBIT: Who is next, Googie?

GOOGIE: It's the boo-hoo bird. I don't know what he can do.

(BOO-HOO *comes out on the stage.*)

MRS. RABBIT: Are you ready, Boo-Hoo?

BOO-HOO: Yes. I'm going to sing a song. Here it is:

(BOO-HOO *is crying as he sings.*)

I'm a little boo-hoo bird.
Boo-hoo! Boo-hoo!
I'd like to sing and dance and play
For you, for you.
I am sad and very blue.
I don't know what I'm going to do.
Boo-hoo! Boo-hoo! Boo-hoo!

GOOGIE: What a sad song! I think I'm going to cry.

MRS. RABBIT: That song makes me sad, too. Our show is going to be a happy show. Your song would make everyone cry. You can't be in the show, Boo-Hoo.

BOO-HOO: I'd better go away and have a good cry. Now I am sad. Good-bye. Boo-hoo-hoo-hoo.

MRS. RABBIT: Don't go too far away. We may think of something you can do.

(BOO-HOO *goes off.*)

GOOGIE: Well, Mrs. Rabbit, so far we have one jumping frog and one funny gorilla.

MRS. RABBIT: We need some more acts for the show, Googie. And we need a star. I'll call some of my friends, and you call some of yours.

GOOGIE: If we don't get some other acts, we can't put on the show.

MRS. RABBIT: And don't forget—we need a name for our show.

(MRS. RABBIT *and* GOOGIE *go off.*)

Act Two

GOOGIE: I wish someone would come soon.

(Knock! Knock! Knock! LITTLE BEAR *comes in.)*

LITTLE BEAR: Boo-Hoo told me about the show, and I want to be in it.

MRS. RABBIT: What can you do?

LITTLE BEAR: I can put on my hat and act like a clown. Are you ready? I'll show you what I can do.

(LITTLE BEAR puts on a clown's mask. He dances about and shows them his funny tricks.)

MRS. RABBIT: What do you think, Googie? Do we need a clown for the show?

GOOGIE: Yes. Every show needs a clown. You can be in the show, Little Bear. Get your clown act ready.

LITTLE BEAR: Can I be the star?

MRS. RABBIT: We'll see about that. Good-bye, Little Bear.

(LITTLE BEAR goes out.)

MRS. RABBIT: Who is next, Googie?

(WOLF comes in before GOOGIE can answer.)

WOLF: I'm next! I'm next! I hear you need a star for your little show and I'm it. I am a star—a BIG star.

GOOGIE:	You are a big bad wolf. We know what you do. You show your teeth and scare everyone.
WOLF:	Not any more, I don't. I'm the good wolf now. I call myself Goody Goody.
MRS. RABBIT:	But what can you do in our show?
WOLF:	What can I DO! I can do EVERYTHING! I can make funny faces. I can jump over boxes. I can sing and I can act like a clown.
MRS. RABBIT:	But can you dance?

WOLF: I can, if I have someone to dance with.

GOOGIE: I think I can find someone to dance with you. What about Boo-Hoo? Let's call him back.

MRS. RABBIT: Yes, that will make him happy.

GOOGIE: Boo-Hoo! Boo-Hoo! You can come back now – but no crying, please, and no sad songs.

(BOO-HOO *comes back.*)

MRS. RABBIT: Goody Goody needs someone to dance with. Will you dance with him?

BOO-HOO: I just happen to have my dancing shoes with me.

GOOGIE: Are you ready to dance, Goody Goody?

WOLF: Yes, I just happen to have my straw hat and my walking stick with me. Come on, Boo-Hoo. Let's dance.

(GOODY GOODY and BOO-HOO dance.)

GOOGIE: They dance very well, don't they? Everyone will like them.

MRS. RABBIT: Boo-Hoo and Goody Goody can be the stars of our show. We'll have a two-star show.

GOOGIE: But Froggie jumps very well and he wants to be a star.

MRS. RABBIT: Then we'll make it a three-star show.

GOOGIE: But what about Gogo? His faces are very funny, and he'll make everyone laugh.

MRS. RABBIT: Why didn't we think of that before? We'll have a four-star show.

GOOGIE: The little bear is very good, too.

MRS. RABBIT: We'll make him a star. We'll have a five-star show.

(BOO-HOO jumps up and down.)

BOO-HOO: I'm so happy I could laugh. Ha! Ha! Ha! Happy days are here again.

GOOGIE: Thank you, Boo-Hoo! That's what we can call our show. Happy Days are Here Again.

MRS. RABBIT: Call in Froggie and Gogo and the little bear. Tell them the good news. Everyone is a star in our show.

(FROGGIE, GOGO, and LITTLE BEAR come in.)

LITTLE BEAR: We know! We know! We could hear you talking. We are all stars. Happy days are here again.

(All the stars do their acts.)

The End

Happy Days Song

Happy days, happy days,
Everyone's a star in Happy Days.
It's a five-star show, and we want you to know
Happy Days are here again!

We'll jump and sing, make faces and laugh,
We'll dance and have a ball.
We'll chase your frowns and tears away-
It's the happiest show of all.

Happy days, happy days,
Everyone's a star in Happy Days.
It's a five-star show, and we want you to know
Happy Days are here again!

Clayton Graves

What You Need to Put on a Play

A script   This tells what everybody in the play says. You can write a script or just make it up.

The stage   This is the part of the room where the play happens. Any part of the room will do. Make sure that everyone can see the stage.

The set   You can paint a background to show where the play happens.

in the woods

on a bus

under the sea

The props   A box can be painted to look like a table. You can make a ball out of newspapers and paint it to look like a rock.

Masks   You can make some masks out of paper. You can also paint a face on a stocking and put it on. You can make papier mache masks with strips of paper and paste. Wool makes a good wig for a mask.

Costumes   You can cut up and paint old clothes. You can sew on big patches to make a clown suit. You can make a robot costume out of boxes covered with tin foil.

Make-up   Use make-up that washes off easily.

Posters   Make posters to tell people about your play. Think of a good name for the play.

Editors
Ruta Demery
Clayton Graves
Barbara Sack

Design
Eccleston & Glossop

Photograph
page 43 Miller Services

Film
Colourgraph

Printing and Binding
McLaren, Morris & Todd

ISBN 0-17-600563-3

9 0 BS/CG 8 6 5 4 3 2 1